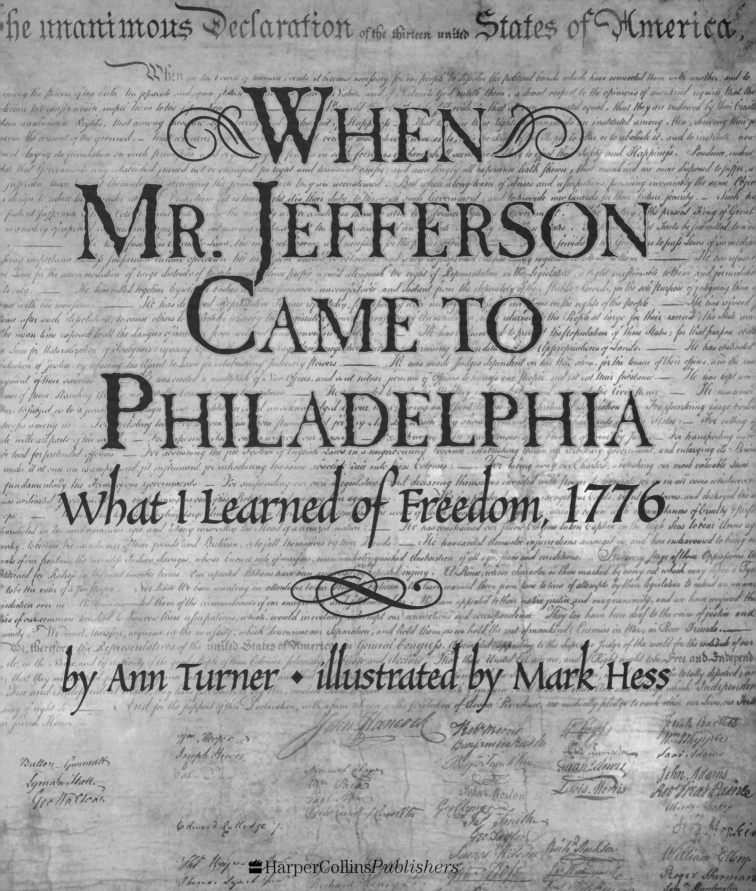

WHEN MR. JEFFERSON CAME TO PHILADELPHIA

What I Learned of Freedom, 1776

by Ann Turner • illustrated by Mark Hess

HarperCollinsPublishers

When Mr. Jefferson Came to Philadelphia:
What I learned of Freedom, 1776
Text copyright © 2003 by Ann Turner
Illustrations copyright © 2003 by Mark Hess
Manufactured in China by South China Printing Company Ltd.
All rights reserved.
www.harperchildrens.com

Library of Congress Cataloging-in-Publication Data
Turner, Ann Warren.
    When Mr. Jefferson came to Philadelphia: what I learned of freedom, 1776 /
by Ann Turner ; illustrated by Mark Hess.
        p.   cm.
    Summary: In Philadelphia in 1776, Ned meets Thomas Jefferson, who is
staying in his mother's inn while debating the topic of freedom in Congress and
writing the Declaration of Independence.
    ISBN 0-06-027579-0. — ISBN 0-06-027580-4 (lib. bdg.)
    1. Jefferson, Thomas, 1743–1826—Juvenile fiction.   2. United States—
History—Revolution, 1775–1783—Juvenile fiction.   [1. Jefferson, Thomas,
1743–1826—Fiction.   2. United States—History—Revolution, 1775–1783—
Fiction.]   I. Hess, Mark, ill.   II. Title.
PZ7.T8535Wh   2003   98-50936
[Fic]—dc21   CIP
                                                                                        AC

Typography by Jeanne L. Hogle
1   2   3   4   5   6   7   8   9   10
❖
First Edition

To my wonderful group of women writers,
who have listened to and encouraged me
in the writing of this book.
—A.T.

I dedicate the paintings in this book to all the
children who enjoy freedom; to all the children
yearning for freedom; and to all the people
who make it possible.
—M.H.

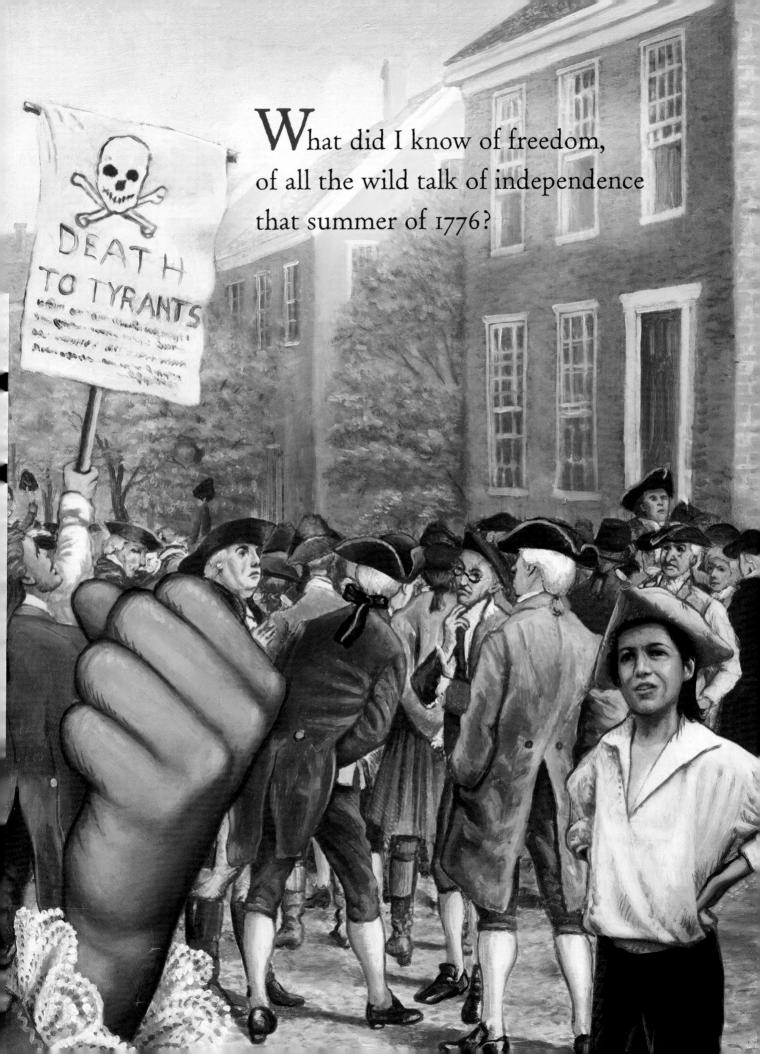

What did I know of freedom, of all the wild talk of independence that summer of 1776?

I was just a boy with jug ears
who tried to stay out of the way.

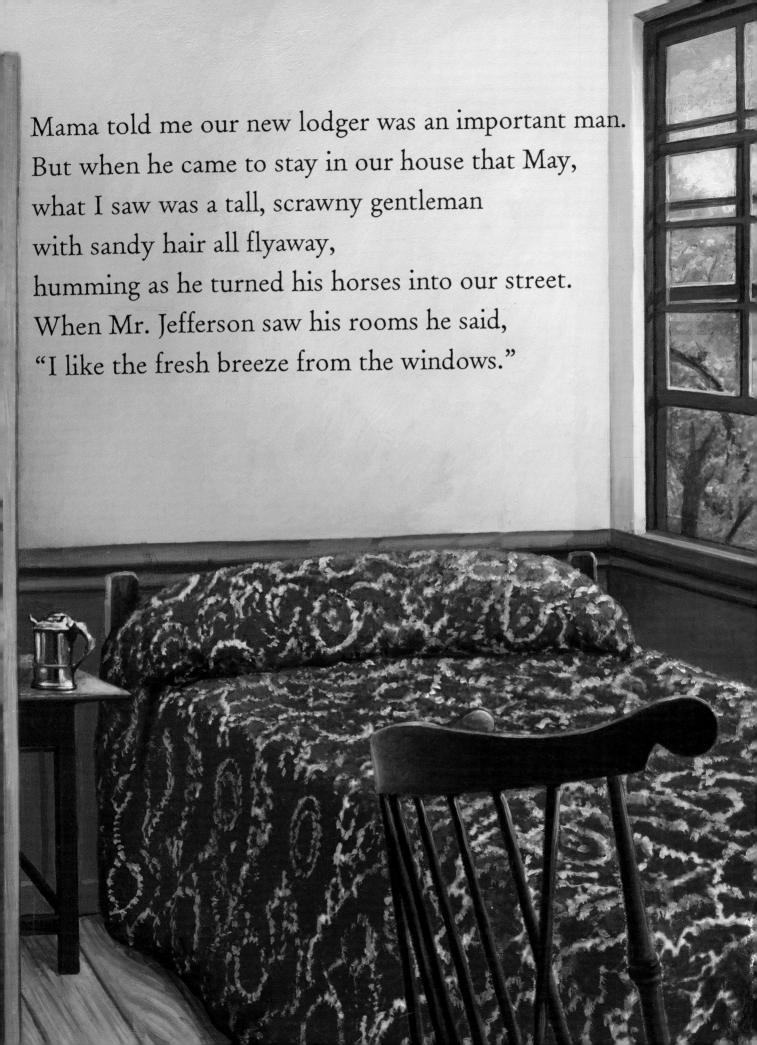

Mama told me our new lodger was an important man.
But when he came to stay in our house that May,
what I saw was a tall, scrawny gentleman
with sandy hair all flyaway,
humming as he turned his horses into our street.
When Mr. Jefferson saw his rooms he said,
"I like the fresh breeze from the windows."

I hoped he would be happy here,
for all these important men
coming to the Congress in Philadelphia
meant money to us,
maybe a new cap for me,
or new shoes for Mama.

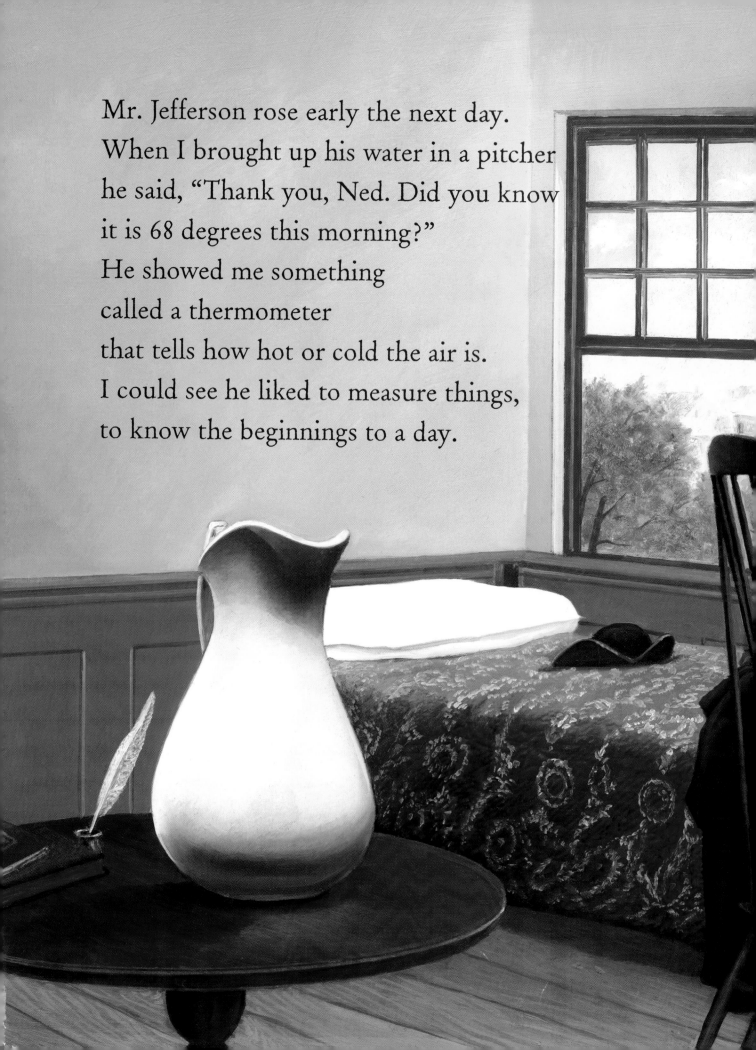

Mr. Jefferson rose early the next day.
When I brought up his water in a pitcher
he said, "Thank you, Ned. Did you know
it is 68 degrees this morning?"
He showed me something
called a thermometer
that tells how hot or cold the air is.
I could see he liked to measure things,
to know the beginnings to a day.

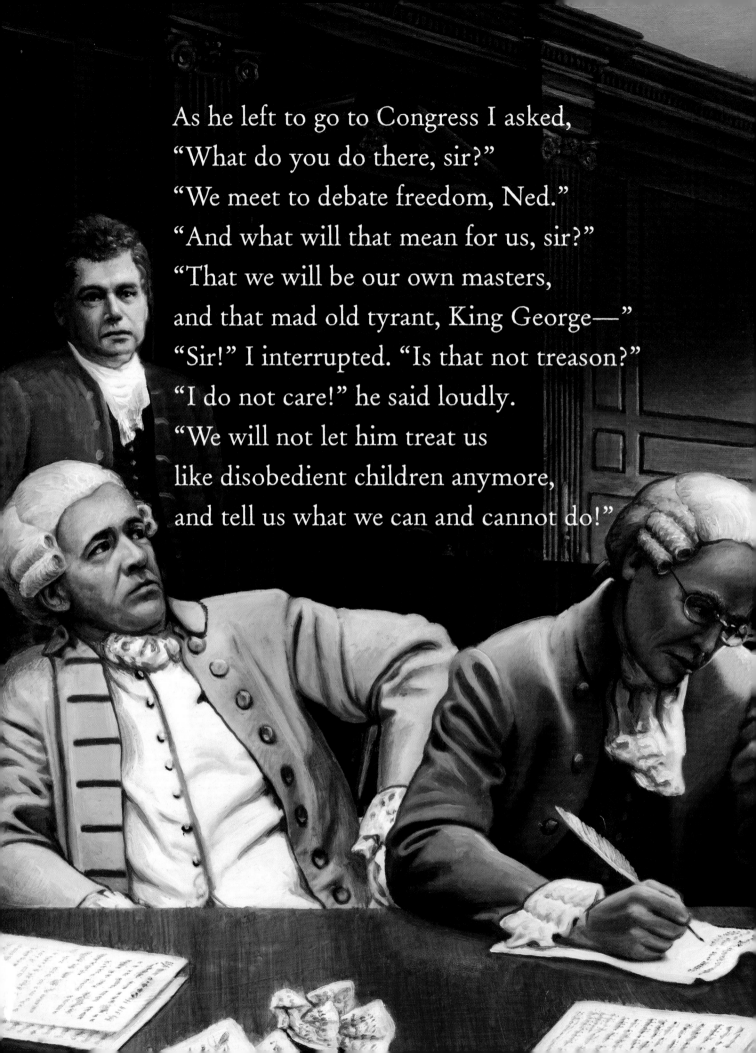

As he left to go to Congress I asked,
"What do you do there, sir?"
"We meet to debate freedom, Ned."
"And what will that mean for us, sir?"
"That we will be our own masters,
and that mad old tyrant, King George—"
"Sir!" I interrupted. "Is that not treason?"
"I do not care!" he said loudly.
"We will not let him treat us
like disobedient children anymore,
and tell us what we can and cannot do!"

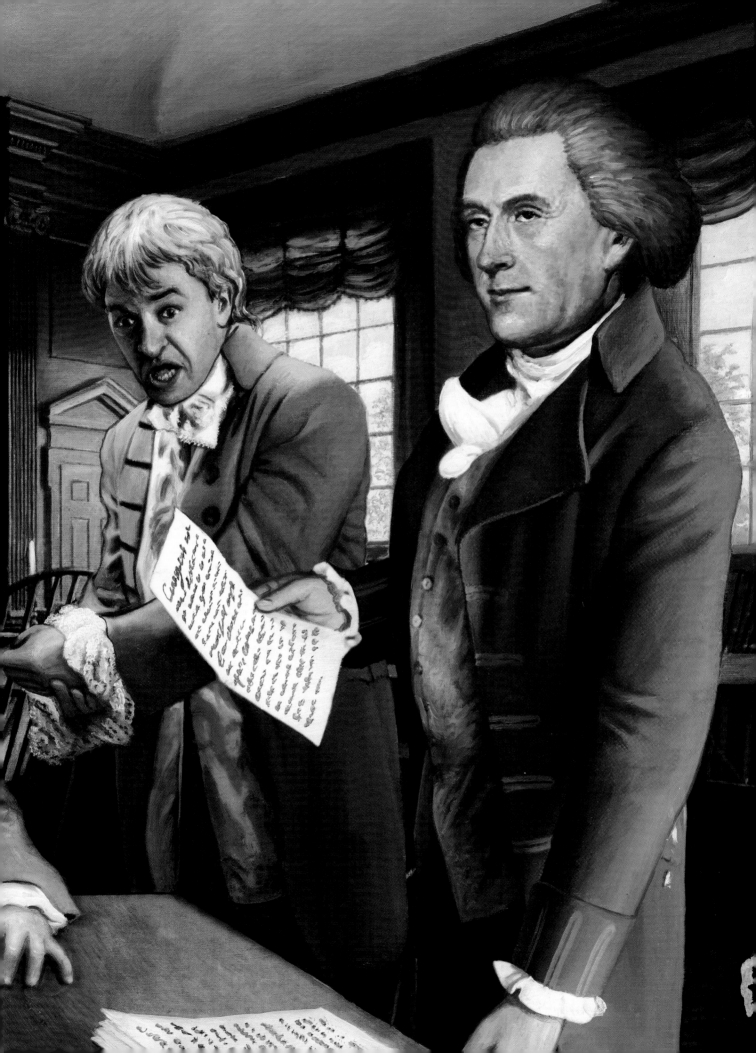

Papa says the penalty for treason
is being hanged by the neck until you are dead.
Wasn't Mr. Jefferson afraid?
That night when I checked the locks outside,
I looked up and saw his light burning,
and Mr. Jefferson writing, writing, writing.

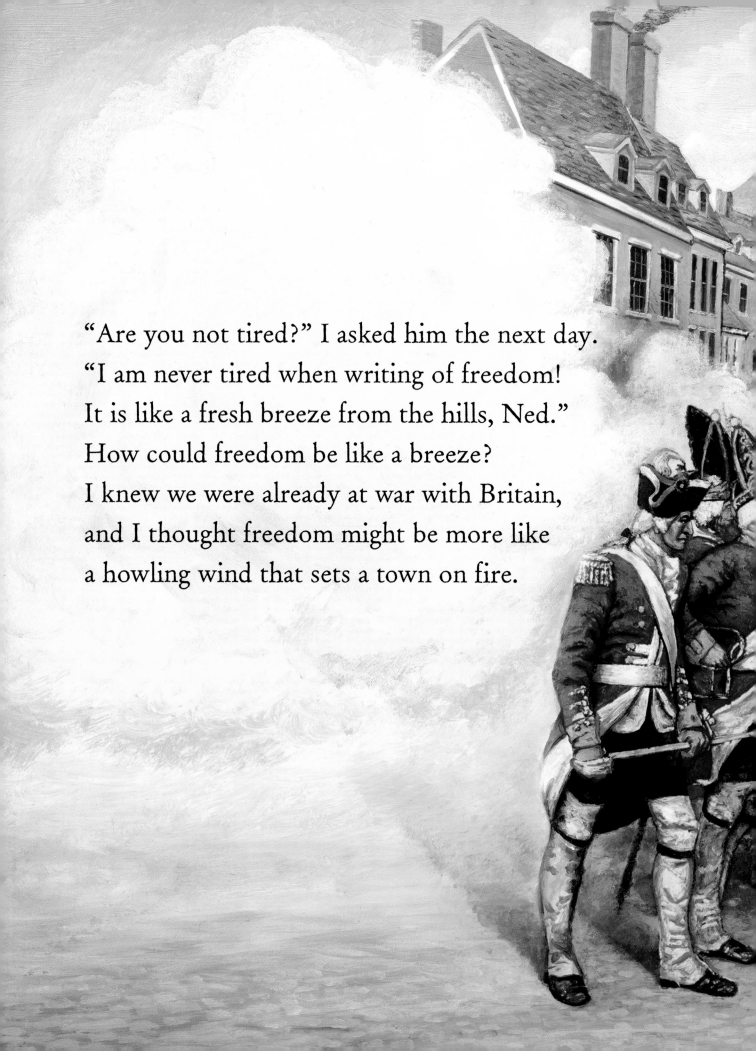

"Are you not tired?" I asked him the next day.
"I am never tired when writing of freedom!
It is like a fresh breeze from the hills, Ned."
How could freedom be like a breeze?
I knew we were already at war with Britain,
and I thought freedom might be more like
a howling wind that sets a town on fire.

One night when I brought him supper
Mr. Jefferson asked, "When you are older
would you fight against the King, Ned?"
I was silent for a moment, and he added,
"So that our colonies can be free and independent?
No one could put unfair taxes on us,
no one could keep foreign soldiers
in our towns and cities."

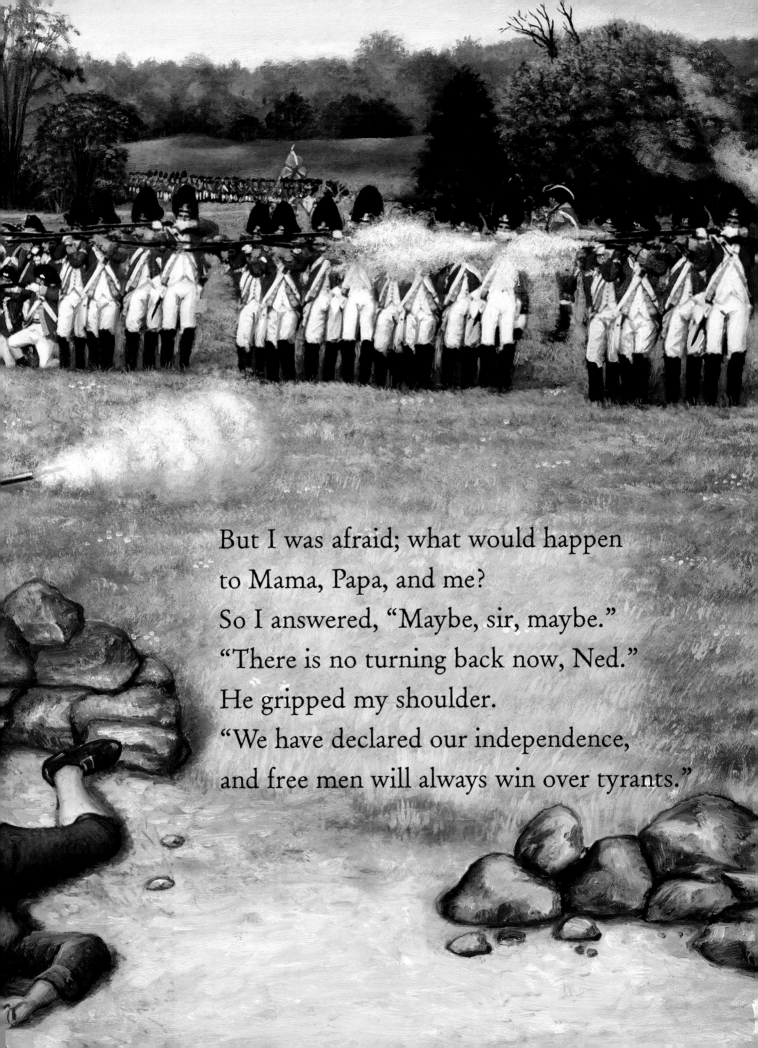

But I was afraid; what would happen
to Mama, Papa, and me?
So I answered, "Maybe, sir, maybe."
"There is no turning back now, Ned."
He gripped my shoulder.
"We have declared our independence,
and free men will always win over tyrants."

I learned more that summer
when we went to the square to hear someone read
the Declaration of Independence.
That was what he had been writing
those nights with the candle burning.

The words were learned and hard,
but they soared up and down like music.
Men and women tossed their caps in the air
and shouted, "Death to the tyrant!"
Even Mama gave a little yell.
There was a wild feeling in the air,
like a fierce wind blowing.
Was this freedom?

The words made my skin shiver up:
    We hold these truths to be self-evident,
    that all men are created equal. . . .
And suddenly I knew he was right,
and had always been right,
and we were cowards not to follow
from the start.

Then I heard something underneath those
words like the beat of a drum. It called to me,
"Freedom, freedom, freedom!
It is coming fast, it will not stop.
Be ready, Ned, be ready."

Historical Note

Shy, tall, with a freckled face and sandy hair. Disliked the rough-and-tumble of political life. Loved fine things and collected them for his mansion, Monticello.

Why would such a man, wealthy and born to an aristocratic family, risk all to fight for freedom from Britain? George Washington said that he and his men fought the war "with halters round their necks." Had the Colonies lost the American Revolution, these leaders would have been hanged and all their lands and estates taken by the King.

But Thomas Jefferson had a vision of freedom and independence, and when he came to Philadelphia in May 1776 for the Second Continental Congress, he already had a reputation for being a radical and a fine writer. He was appointed to a committee to write a document arguing for independence.

He had some hard tasks ahead of him: to persuade the colonists to vote for independence, while many wished to remain joined to Britain; to list the wrongs of Britain against the colonies; and to give a vision of the future of America without a king.

Although the other four men on the committee—his friends Benjamin Franklin and John Adams, along with Robert Sherman and Robert Livingston—did make suggestions and some revisions, Thomas Jefferson wrote the Declaration of Independence himself in only a few days.

It was debated in Congress in early July and approved on July Fourth, the day we celebrate independence. Congress had an important role in tightening and shaping the Declaration, although Jefferson always regretted those changes.

In his early years, Jefferson's vision of freedom did include the black slaves of the Colonies. He wished them to be freed. But as time went on, his support for this position waned, and he wrote that it would be up to the next generation to deal with the problem.

While Jefferson longed to see "this ball of liberty roll round the globe," he still kept slaves. We may find it hard to understand how he could talk of freedom and be a slaveholder. But across the years his beautiful and impassioned words still call to us:

We hold these truths to be self-evident,
that all men are created equal. . . .

They are words that we still must work to live up to.

NOTE 1: This is not meant to be a comprehensive discussion of Thomas Jefferson's accomplishments, which were legion. I am indebted to these sources for their contribution to my understanding of this complex man and his times:

Joseph J. Ellis, *American Sphinx: The Character of Thomas Jefferson.*
Fawn M. Brodie, *Thomas Jefferson, an Intimate History.*
Pauline Maier, *American Scripture: Making the Declaration of Independence.*

Note 2: Regarding pages 12–13, we know that Jefferson recorded the temperature as 68 degrees on July 4, 1776. We don't know for certain that he brought a thermometer with him to Philadelphia, but think it likely, as it was a habit of his to mark down temperature readings. We do know he bought a new thermometer on that very day, and we leave it to you to solve this mystery.